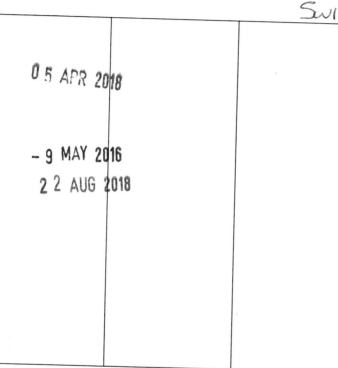

First published in Great Britain in 2017 by Simon & Schuster UK Ltd
A CBS COMPANY

1 3 5 7 9 10 8 6 4 2

Simon & Schuster UK Ltd
1st Floor, 222 Gray's Inn Road
London
WC1X 8HB

www.simonandschuster.co.uk
www.simonandschuster.com.au
www.simonandschuster.co.in

Simon & Schuster Australia, Sydney
Simon & Schuster India, New Delhi

A CIP catalogue record for this book is available from the British Library.

PB ISBN: 978-1-4711-6090-5
eBook ISBN: 978-1-4711-6091-2

Printed and bound by CPI Group (UK) Ltd, Croydon, CR0 4YY

KAYE UMANSKY

Witch
for a
Week

Illustrated by
ASHLEY KING

For Freya, Elinor,
Reuben and Erin

PICKLES' TOP TEN RULES
OF CUSTOMER SERVICE

1. BE FRIENDLY
2. PRETEND THAT THE CUSTOMER
   IS ALWAYS RIGHT
3. BE A GOOD LISTENER
4. KEEP PEOPLE CHATTING
5. BE SYMPATHETIC
6. USE A SOOTHING TONE WITH THE
   TRICKY ONES
7. ALWAYS BE HELPFUL
8. STAY OPEN WHENEVER POSSIBLE
9. ALWAYS HAVE A HANDY HANKY
10. USE FLATTERY

Chapter One
THE WITCH BLOWS IN

Elsie Pickles was minding the family shop when the witch blew into town.

The town was called Smallbridge, because it was small and had a bridge. The bridge spanned a sluggish river called the Dribble. Like the river, life in Smallbridge trickled on with calm monotony. It was a dull little town where people went to bed early because there was nothing else to do.

The shop was just off the main street, down

a narrow alley, and was called, rather grandly, Pickles' Emporium. But it wasn't grand at all. It was dark and dingy and sold cheap, boring things. Tea strainers. Buckets. Candles. Boot polish. Paper clips. The till didn't ding much. In fact, mostly people just came in to chat and didn't spend a penny. Some weeks, the shop hardly brought in enough to put food on the Pickles' table.

This particular day was a sunny Saturday. The high street was thronged with shoppers, strollers, children, chickens and the odd wandering pig. Smallbridge's stray dog lay sprawled in the middle of it all, tripping people up and enjoying the morning sun.

The Emporium was doing its usual roaring trade. Elsie had sold a shoelace. Her dad had sold a mop. Both of them had listened to a

lot of moaning about bad backs and annoying neighbours. Just another day of poor sales and earache. Nothing out of the ordinary at all.

And then . . .

The town hall clock struck twelve. High noon.

The last chime died away . . .

And everything changed!

A wind came howling out of nowhere, sending hats flying and rubbish skittering along the cobbles. This wind wasn't a summer breeze. This wind was ferocious. The sort of wind that could uproot trees and topple chimneys.

The high street emptied as everyone ran for cover, holding down skirts and grabbing for flying parasols. Shopkeepers battled to pull down shutters. Children were called in. Doors slammed. The stray dog disappeared. It was like that moment in a western films when the gunslinger comes to town and everyone runs for safety.

'Look at that,' said Elsie's dad. 'Weather's turned. I doubt we'll have many customers now. Reckon I'll put me feet up for five minutes.'

'Shall I put up the **CLOSED** sign?' asked Elsie.

'Nope. Remember Customer Service Rule Eight: Stay Open Whenever Possible. You'll be all right on your own, won't you? Make us our fortune, love.'

I wish, thought Elsie, as he trudged upstairs.

All they needed was one rich customer who was crazy about cheap, boring stuff. Although, now Elsie thought about it, she didn't suppose the Emporium's entire stock was worth much at all.

Outside, the wind continued to rage about

the deserted streets, looking for things to push over. Rich or poor, there would be no customers out in this wild, weird weather.

Elsie gave a small sigh. She loved Mum and Dad, and her three little brothers, Arthy, Toby and baby Todd. And she didn't really mind working in the shop. But sometimes she wished that her life was a little more exciting, like in books.

Elsie loved reading. She had read almost all the books in Smallbridge's tiny library. She couldn't bring them home because the boys would always ruin them. But she knew the best stories by heart.

Of course, in books, it was almost always the youngest son who had the adventures and made the fortune. Girls in stories mostly danced or slept, passing time until a prince came to the rescue, and then they would get married in big white dresses and beautiful shoes. None of them worked in shops.

Elsie hopped up on the counter and stared down at her battered old boots. She imagined her own feet in beautiful shoes. Blue ones, with ribbons. She had seen the perfect pair in the cobbler's window. May Day was coming soon and Smallbridge always had a street parade to celebrate with music and dancing. Oh, how she would love those blue shoes! Sadly, it was an impossible dream. Unlike the storybook princesses, she couldn't afford them.

No harm in wishing, though, thought Elsie.

There came a sudden, sharp tap on the window. Elsie looked up.

And there she was. The witch. Staring through the glass. Green eyes in a pale face. Strands of wild auburn hair whipping wildly around her head.

For a long moment, she held Elsie's startled gaze . . .

Then she was gone.

Crash! The door flew open! The rusty old doorbell fell to the floor and shattered!

The wind barged in, swept round, saw nothing it wanted and roared back out again!

And suddenly the witch was in the shop.

Elsie had heard all the gossip about this strange customer. Magenta Sharp was her name, and the villagers called her the Red Witch for three reasons:

1. HER RED HAIR

2. THE RED GLOVES SHE ALWAYS WORE

3. HER RED CLOAK AND MATCHING POINTY BOOTS

Even if she hadn't been a witch, people would have talked about Magenta Sharp, because she hadn't been born and bred in Smallbridge and was therefore a bit suspect. She rarely came to town – only when she needed the sole of a boot fixing or to buy some socks – one of those dull errands that you put off for as long as possible. When she did visit, she didn't go out of her way to make herself popular. Just swept in and out again, ignoring everyone and tapping her foot impatiently if she was kept waiting.

Whenever she arrived, there was always bad weather. Sudden snowfalls, hail, thick fog. Annoying weather that people were never suitably dressed for. The more traditional townsfolk were also put out by the fact she always dressed in those dreadful, garish red clothes! She didn't shuffle about in black rags and the traditional pointy hat, like a respectable witch would. Not a cackle to be heard. Not a wart to be seen. No sign of a broomstick. She was different. Strange. Unwelcome.

People said she lived in a tower deep in Crookfinger Forest, although nobody had actually seen it. Everyone avoided the forest. It grew right up to the edge of town and was vast, ancient and a bit frightening. The sort of place that might hide dark secrets.

Many rumours had grown up about the tower. Some said it was made of glass. Some said ice. Some said marble. They said it was impossible to find – in which case, of course, they wouldn't have a clue what it was made of. When Elsie pointed that out, they just shrugged their shoulders and said, 'Still . . .' in a meaningful way.

None of that mattered to Elsie, though. What mattered was that here was a customer who just might spend some money.

Elsie jumped down, took her place at the till, put on a welcoming smile and said brightly: 'Can I help?'

Chapter Two
ANYONE COULD DO IT

The witch nudged the broken bell with the toe of her boot.

'You need a new bell.'

She said it abruptly, as though she had nothing to do with it. No 'sorry, was that me?' No 'oh dear, allow me to pay for the damage'. Nothing.

'So we do,' agreed Elsie. 'Never mind, accidents happen. See anything you fancy?'

'Frankly,' said the witch, staring round the tiny shop, 'no.'

'Well, take your time. Corkscrews are on sale today and we have a special offer on hinges. It's a nasty wind out, isn't it?'

Saying these kind of things is automatic when you work in a shop. Elsie's dad had taught her all the important rules of Customer Service. Things like:

1) BE FRIENDLY, EVEN TO RUDE PEOPLE

(in fact, especially to rude people)

2) PRETEND THAT THE CUSTOMER IS ALWAYS RIGHT

(even when they're clearly wrong)

3) BE A GOOD LISTENER AND MAKE SURE TO NOD AND LOOK INTERESTED

(not easy when talking about corkscrews and hinges)

4) KEEP PEOPLE CHATTING AND THEY JUST MIGHT BUY SOMETHING

And those were just the top four; her dad had hundreds of rules! Elsie was very good at Customer Service.

'I brought the wind with me,' said the witch. 'Thought things could do with a bit of a shake-up round here, it's always so deadly dull, don't you think?'

'I do,' said Elsie, Customer Service Rules One, Three and Four clicking in. 'Nothing like a bit of wild weather to stir people up. They'll moan about it for weeks.'

'Good. My efforts are not in vain. Where's your noticeboard?'

'Behind you.' Elsie pointed.

'How much to display this?' A large piece of paper suddenly appeared in the witch's red-gloved hand.

'A penny for the week,' said Elsie.

'I haven't got a week. I need fast results.'

'It's still a penny, I'm afraid. But I'll point it out to people, of course.' (Customer Service Rule Seven: Always Be Helpful.) 'Are you sure I can't tempt you with a half-price kitchen mat?' (Customer Service Rule Eleven: Draw Attention to a Bargain.)

'No.' The witch snapped her fingers. 'Pins.'

Elsie handed over four drawing pins and the witch fastened the piece of paper slap bang in the middle of the board, knocking down several old notices in the process.

'"Temporary Caretaker Wanted",' read Elsie. '"Apply to Magenta Sharp. Tower in Forest." Hmmm . . .'

'What do you mean, "hmmm"?' The witch frowned. 'Something wrong?'

'Well, you need a bit more information.'

'Such as?'

'Such as, how long do you need someone for?'

'A week. I'm visiting my sister. Although if she's like she is sometimes, I could be back in a matter of hours.'

'When would you want someone to start?'

'Tomorrow.'

'That's very short notice. What will the duties be?'

'Lock up. Keep nosy parkers at bay. Take in the complaints.'

'Complaints?'

'I run a mail order service. **Sharp Spells on Tap**.' The witch sniffed. 'Wish I'd never started it. I spend all my time wrapping up parcels that leak, explode or never arrive. People moan and want refunds.'

'Poor you,' said Elsie sympathetically. 'People can be so unreasonable, can't they?'

Be Sympathetic was Customer Service Rule Five. But in this case, Elsie was genuinely interested. The witch was very different to the usual Emporium customer.

'Yes,' said the witch. 'They can. Oh! Almost forgot. The caretaker will need to change Corbett's water.'

'Who's Corbett?'

'The raven. Comes with the tower. Looks after himself mostly, but turning the tap on is a step too far. No opposable thumbs, you see.'

'Corbett's an unusual name,' said Elsie. 'If I had a raven, I'd call him Charlie.'

'It means *raven* in Old French. But I didn't name him, it's what he's called.'

'Right,' said Elsie. 'Change Corbett's water. Is that it?'

'Pretty much. There's no need to cook, the tower takes care of that. I've got a decent collection of books, for anyone who's interested.' Her eyes narrowed. 'You like reading, don't you? I've seen you in the library. Go there often?'

'Not as much as I'd like,' said Elsie. 'I'm usually stuck here in the shop. And I can't bring books home. My little brothers chew them.'

'Well, stop them! Freeze them in their tracks! I have a spell for that. Comes in

spray form. **Squeeze 'n' Freezem**. One squirt and they're rigid. It's one of my more popular products.'

'I'm sure,' said Elsie. 'But I don't think it's very nice to freeze family.'

'I don't see why not. I've done a lot worse to my sister. But here's another clever suggestion. Put the books out of the way.'

'There's nowhere to hide them. We're very squashed upstairs. Erm, just to be clear, the caretaker's duties wouldn't involve any actual . . . *magical* activity, would they?'

'No. All professional services are on hold until I get back. Of course, the tower's got all the *magical* gear – fully equipped, so to speak. So, if the fancy took, there's nothing wrong with having a little *dabble*. Trying out a spell or two, just for the fun of it. I'm a great believer in letting people have a go at things. How else will they know if they're any good?'

'Isn't that dangerous?' asked Elsie. 'Going off and leaving someone to mess about with spells and stuff if they don't know what they're doing?'

'Ah. You're talking health and safety. I don't bother with all that.' The witch leaned her sharp elbows on the counter. 'You learn by your mistakes, Elsie. Besides, if you stick to the rules, magic is surprisingly straightforward. People don't realize that.'

'How do you know my na—'

'*Shush,* I'm talking. There are three important things to remember when it comes to magic.' The witch ticked them off on her long red fingers. 'One, read the instructions. Two, follow the recipe. Three, make it work.'

'I was with you until the last one,' said Elsie.

'How do you "make it work"?'

'Practise. It helps to have the knack, of course.'

'The knack?'

'Yes. It's like playing the piano, or creating a delicious meal out of cheese rind, an old potato and a stick of rhubarb. Some have it, some don't.' She straightened up. 'Anyway. Back to business. Anything else you think I need to put in the advert?'

'It would help to say how much you're paying.'

'Haven't a clue. What do you think?'

'I don't know. Just what's fair.'

'Very well. I shall pay what's fair.' The witch gave Elsie a sideways look. 'Plenty enough for a new pair of pretty blue shoes, I would think.'

Elsie was shocked.

Shoes? she thought. *How does she know about my dream blue shoes?*

'That's what you want, isn't it?'

'Well, yes. But how . . . ?'

'Oh, stop gaping like a fish. I'm a witch! Mind-reading is part of my skill set. If you want your thoughts to remain private, don't leave shoes lying around where anyone can trip over them. Anyway, the job's a piece of cake if you can put up with Corbett. *You* could do it.'

'Me? Oh, no,' said Elsie. 'No, I have to help Dad in the shop. And Mum needs help with my brothers.'

'It'd help if you could earn enough for new boots for your brothers, wouldn't it? Provide a turkey for May Day? New bonnet for your mother? Bit of extra cash, smarten the shop up? Mmm?'

'They won't agree,' said Elsie.

'Because I'm a witch, I suppose. They're witchist.'

'They're not! They don't know you, that's all.'

'So? I won't be there.'

'Even so, Dad won't let me.'

'I have a spell for that. Yes Drops. Three drops in his tea and he'll agree to anything. Kiss a frog. Eat his own socks.'

'I said that I don't think you should use spells on family,' said Elsie.

'Fine, do it the long way, if you must. Get your mother on side. Talk up the turkey. Big up the bonnet. Tell her you'll be safely back home in seven days, she has my word. Think of it, Elsie. Your own bedroom. Plenty of interesting books to read. Time to yourself. And I will pay you – let me see – twenty-one gold pieces, three for each day. The traditional purse of gold. Fair?'

Elsie was taken aback. Twenty-one gold pieces? Why, that was a fortune! More than

Pickles' Emporium had earned in the last ten years!

But . . .

'What are you waiting for, Elsie?' the witch pressed. 'Where's your sense of adventure? I know you've got one.'

She's right, thought Elsie. *I have.*

But . . .

'Come early tomorrow morning. Bring a toothbrush. Here's your penny for the advert – use it to buy a new bell.'

A coin appeared in her hand. It leapt up, spun through the air and landed on its edge on the counter before rolling to the till, ready to be popped in.

'How will I find you?' asked Elsie. It was out of her mouth before she could help it. 'Not that I'm saying I'll do it, but . . .'

'Walk into Crookfinger Forest and keep going. We'll find *you*.'

And with that, the witch was gone. Not through the door. Just – gone.

Outside, the wind dropped. A shaft of sunlight streamed through the window. There came the sound of rumbling wheels and hesitant feet as the town rose back to life.

Elsie scooped up the coin and rang up the till . . .

Which was full to the brim with shiny copper pennies!

Chapter Three
CROOKFINGER FOREST

Very early the next morning, Elsie walked out of Smallbridge. She had said her goodbyes the night before, and crept out while the family was sleeping.

It had taken a fair amount of talking to get her mum and dad to agree – but her Customer Service skills made Elsie a very good talker. The till full of pennies helped too. And, of course, there is something about the words 'purse of gold' that is very persuasive.

The town's stray dog was known as Nuisance, because he was. This morning he was definitely living up to his name. His main talent was tripping people up, but right now he was being annoying in another way. He was following her. Sometime last year, Elsie had given him half a sausage. He was still hoping for the other half.

'Go home, Nuisance,' ordered Elsie, but immediately felt bad. He didn't have a home.

Nuisance didn't take offence. He wagged his tattered tail, trying to look like a winsome puppy you might feed half a sausage to, rather than a disintegrating piece of old carpet.

'Go on,' said Elsie. 'I haven't any food.' This was true. Her basket just contained her toothbrush and a change of underwear. And, at her mum's insistence, a warm shawl.

'Write home the minute you get there,

mind,' her mum had said.

'I don't think there'll be a postbox in the forest,' Elsie had said.

'She's a witch, isn't she? Tell her to magic one up. If we don't hear in a day or two, Dad's coming to find you.'

Elsie didn't think that was very likely. Crookfinger Forest was no sun-speckled wood. It was old, dark and scary and it went on forever. Nobody walked dogs there, or went looking for blackberries. Children were forbidden to venture into the trees. And the forest was full of wolves. At night, you could hear them howling.

Elsie gazed into the wall of dark trees. There was no proper path to follow. No gates or signposts.

'We'll find you.' Those had been the witch's words.

Right, thought Elsie, *Plunge in and hope for the best. That's how most adventures start.*

'Bye, Nuisance,' she said. 'Wish me luck.'

To begin with, the forest was surprisingly pleasant. Birds sang overhead, and here and there were bunches of bluebells. Elsie considered picking some for the witch, but decided against it. Hanging about picking flowers wasn't a good idea. Not that Elsie believed in talking wolves who ate grandmothers, of course.

But when you were alone in a forest, it was a story you didn't want to think about.

She continued on, following an old badger track, trying to imagine what it would be like to live alone. Looking after herself wouldn't be a problem. She helped her mum cook, clean and scrub clothes at home, in the tiny attic above the shop that was hardly big enough for one person, let alone six. And the idea of sleeping in a bed of her own was so exciting! No elbows in her ribs or feet in her face. Elsie loved Arthy, Toby and baby Todd, but sharing a bed with three small brothers was no fun at all.

She thought about the books the witch had mentioned. Imagine being able to sit and read for hours on end without being disturbed!

She wondered what was meant by the tower

having all the magical 'gear'. Not that it mattered. Elsie didn't intend to try any magic. In stories, when people messed about with spells, things always went horribly wrong.

As she walked further and further into the forest, Elsie stopped thinking. She needed all her concentration to keep going. The badger trail had long vanished. Now there were potholes, fallen branches and thick roots. The trees grew so close that their branches intertwined, blocking the light. Thorn bushes dragged at her cloak. Nettles stung her legs.

Even worse, she kept thinking she could hear something behind her – heavy breathing and the occasional crack of a twig. Things were no longer exciting. Things were scary.

Heart beating fast, Elsie came to a halt in a small glade and peered around in the gloom.

'Hello?' she called. 'Anyone there? Miss Sharp? It's me, Elsie!'

Her voice echoed away into silence. Somewhere high above, a bird flapped away, screeching. And then:

'Over here,' came a voice. 'Behind you.'

Elsie turned around.

And there it was! The tower. Soaring high above the trees, it was neither glass nor ice. It was built of common grey stone, and covered in a thick coat of ivy, which made it blend in to its surroundings. Shuttered windows studded the four walls. At the very top, catching the morning sun, fluttered a red flag.

It hadn't been there a moment ago, Elsie was sure of it. Ivy or not, you couldn't miss something like that.

The witch stood on the step, her back to the

door, a carpet bag in one hand. There was no sign of her usual red cloak; instead she wore a neat grey travelling coat. Her hair was scraped back into a tidy bun. Apart from the red gloves, she looked almost normal.

'Sorry we're late,' she said. 'I was busy making myself look respectable. Do I?'

'Very,' said Elsie.

'They're stuffy, where my sister lives. I'm supposed to "blend in". She tells people I'm a librarian. No problem getting your parents to agree you could stay here?'

'Oh, no. Not really. The till being full of pennies helped. Thank you for that, Miss Sharp.'

'Magenta will do. Come in, I'll run over the basics of the job with you. I haven't long. I'm catching the early coach. I'd use a transportation spell, but my sister prefers me to arrive in a

conventional manner.'

Elsie was about to put her foot on the step when Magenta said: 'Wait. Introductions first. Elsie – Tower. Tower – Elsie.'

There was a pause. Elsie wasn't sure what to expect. Thunder? A big, booming voice? Would the tower bend over and shake her hand?

The door opened. Just quietly opened. No squeak. No fuss.

'Right,' said Magenta. 'It seems happy enough. Come on in.'

Chapter Four
EVERYTHING YOU NEED TO KNOW

Elsie looked around the tower, taking in her new home for the week. A flight of stone steps wound up into shadow. To her right, a low archway led into a small, cosy kitchen. A rocking chair sat before a fireplace where a cauldron hung suspended. There was a table with two more chairs, a stove and a sink. Shelves and cupboards lined the walls. Herbs hung from hooks in the rafters. A clock ticked on the wall. One corner was given over to a wooden perch, on which hunched a large black raven.

Elsie knew nothing about birds, but this one didn't look friendly.

'This is Corbett,' said Magenta. 'Corbett, meet Elsie.'

The raven raised his head and stared. Despite only having two eyes and a beak to work with, somehow he managed to arrange them into a sneer. Then he turned his back.

'Sulking,' explained Magenta. 'In a strop because he can't come with me.'

'Oh, is that right? I don't *think* so!' came a hoarse rasp from the perch.

'Yes, you are!'

'Oh!' Elsie was startled. 'You didn't mention that he talked.'

'All the time.' Magenta sniffed. 'He's got

opinions on *everything*. That's right, Corbett, you carry on sulking, at least it means you're quiet.' She turned to Elsie. 'I've tried spells to shut him up but the tower overrides them. It's one of the Ancient Rules.'

'*Shut Thou Not the Raven's Beak. Ravens Have the Right To Speak,*' quoted Corbett.

Elsie wasn't sure, but she thought she felt the slightest of vibrations from the surrounding walls.

'He can't leave the tower, you see,' went on Magenta. 'That's another rule.'

'*Bad Luck Will Come to Stay Should the Raven Fly Away,*' recited Corbett, adding, 'So be warned. If I go, you're in deep trouble.' Again there came that faint vibration. 'See? The tower agrees.'

'Oh, stop your doomy nonsense,' snapped

Magenta. 'Ignore him, Elsie. Moody old misery.'

'I'm sure we'll get on fine,' said Elsie.

'I doubt it,' said Corbett.

'We will if you want fresh water,' said Elsie. 'I hear you can't work the tap.'

Corbett mumbled something under his breath which sounded a lot like: 'May pigeons poop on your silly head!' Then he put his head under a wing and pretended to go to sleep.

'Now,' said Magenta briskly, 'I can't stop to show you round. You'll have plenty of time to explore. But don't worry, I'm leaving you a book. It's all in there. How things work. Where things are. What to do in an emergency. Not that there will be one.'

She opened a drawer and took out a square, thick book with a red cover. Written on the front in bold, black capitals were the words:

With a certain amount of pride, she placed it on the table.

'I was up all night writing it. I think you'll find it very useful.' She pointed to a ring of keys on a hook. 'Keys for all the rooms. Make sure *all* the doors are locked at night and when you go out. Any questions?'

'One thing,' said Elsie. 'The tower. I couldn't help noticing, it . . . well . . . it wasn't there. And then it . . . was.'

'Yes. We like to move around from time to time. When the neighbours get annoying, or if we don't want to be found.'

Elsie thought about this.

'It won't move by itself, will it?' she asked. 'While I'm asleep, or something?'

'No. I've set it to long-term parking. Any more questions?'

Elsie had plenty, but Magenta was clearly in a hurry, so she contented herself by saying: 'You have neighbours?'

'I do. I wouldn't advise inviting them in as they tend to outstay their welcome. Especially not the Howler Sisters. They're light-fingered.'

'Right,' said Elsie, nodding. 'No Howlers allowed.'

'The woodcutter will be along tomorrow to cut more logs for the fire. His name's Hank. If you get cold, the log pile is out the back, next to the privy. I pay him sixpence. There's loose change in the jar on the mantelpiece.'

'Got it,' said Elsie.

'Then there's Aggie Wiggins – or Sylphine Greenmantle, as she's started calling herself.

She dresses like a wood sprite, usually got some wretched animal in tow, so you'll know her as soon as you see her.'

'Okay,' said Elsie. 'Um – why does she dress like a wood sprite?'

'She thinks she looks romantic. Ridiculous, but you can't tell some people. Wherever Hank goes, she's not far behind, silly soppy girl. But it's all in the book. Plenty more reading matter up in the office. Help yourself. Right, I'm off. See you in seven days, if I last that long.'

Magenta marched to the door and picked up her bag.

'Have a lovely time,' said Elsie.

'We'll see. Don't let the dog in unless he's had a bath.'

'What dog?'

'The one hiding under a bush, hoping for half

a sausage. Goodbye, then. Have a nice, quiet time.'

And with that, she vanished. One moment there, the next, gone.

Elsie stared out at the trees.

'How?' she muttered. 'How does she *do* that?'

A breeze blew through the treetops. A faint voice replied: 'I have a spell for that . . .'

Chapter Five
TAILS

'Come out, Nuisance,' called Elsie. 'I know you're there.'

The dog came lolloping from the undergrowth, his coat a matted mass of burrs, leaves and twigs.

'Wait there,' said Elsie. 'I'll see what there is to eat.'

Corbett's unfriendly black eyes followed her as she crossed the kitchen and began opening cupboards.

'Tall door next to the sink,' he growled.

'Oh, good,' said Elsie. 'You're speaking now, are you?'

'Anything to stop you banging about. Making my head ache.'

Elsie opened the larder door and gasped. She had never seen so much food! Eggs, ham, cheese, tomatoes, a loaf of bread, biscuits, a jug of fresh milk, apples – everything she loved! Plus a cake! A beautiful iced cake, with a pink ribbon!

She filled a bowl with water, took a biscuit, went to the door and set them down on the outside step.

'Here. I'll cut you some cheese later.'

Nuisance downed the biscuit in one and thirstily lapped at the water, then flopped on the ground and scratched happily at his fleas.

Elsie went back inside and helped herself to

an apple and a glass of milk.

'Anything for you?' she asked Corbett. 'Biscuit? Breadcrumbs? How's your water dish?'

'My water dish is fine. And I only consume natural food. Insects. Worms. Bread's for common pigeons who don't know any better.' Corbett paused for a moment, then burst out, 'We don't *need* you here, you know. Me and the tower. We're quite *capable* of managing on our own!'

'Of course you are,' said Elsie soothingly. (Customer Service Rule Six: Use a Soothing Tone with Tricky Customers.) 'It's just the water thing, I suppose.'

'I am completely self-sufficient and I prefer my own company.'

'Well, I won't bother you,' said Elsie. 'I'm looking forward to some peace and quiet too. You get the worms yourself, I take it?'

'I do.'

'I thought you couldn't leave the tower.'

'I can't *fly* away. Meaning long distance. I can go for short, local journeys. Don't you know anything, girl?'

'No,' said Elsie. 'Not yet. But hopefully reading this will help.' She walked to the table, where *Everything You Need to Know* waited. She sat down, took a bite of apple and a sip of milk.

'May penguins peck your mother! They're here already,' Corbett groaned before she could even open the book.

'What? Who?' Elsie asked.

'The Howlers. Get rid of 'em.'

'Cooo-eee!' called a voice from the doorway. 'Anybody in?'

Elsie went to the door and saw two little old ladies smiling up at her. One wore a blue dress, the other pink, but apart from that they were identical, both with tight grey curls and kindly faces. They had matching parasols and carried a basket each. Elsie thought they looked sweet and harmless. Like perfect grandmothers.

Nuisance didn't think so. He was sitting bolt upright on the step, growling and showing the whites of his eyes.

'Can I help you?' asked Elsie.

'Is Magenta there, dear?' asked the one in blue.

'No, I'm afraid not. She's away for a few days.'

'Oh? She didn't say, did she, Ada?'

'No, Evie,' said the pink one. 'Not a word.'

'I'm Elsie. I'm looking after things while she's away.'

'Well, dear, we're good friends of Magenta's,' said Evie. 'Can we come in?'

'I'm afraid it's not a good time. I've just arrived, you see.'

'We won't stay long, dear,' said Ada. She stared at Nuisance, who bared his teeth. 'If you

could just get the nice doggy to move.'

'Perhaps another time,' said Elsie. 'Right now, I'm rather busy, I'm afraid.'

'Well, maybe we can help, dear. We're very good at unpacking,' said Evie.

There came a sudden, hoarse squawk from the kitchen.

'Oi! Girl! Get in here! Something's burning!'

'Sorry, got to go!' said Elsie.

'That's a shame,' said Ada. 'Tomorrow, maybe?'

'Maybe,' said Elsie. 'Thank you for calling.'

'You're welcome, dear,' they chorused.

Arm in arm, the sisters turned and walked away.

Elsie gasped as she saw what was protruding from slits in the back of each of their skirts . . .

Chapter Six
SYLPHINE

'Tails!' said Elsie, coming back to the kitchen. 'They've got *tails*. They *wagged!*'

'Yes,' said Corbett. 'Extra feature, all part of their charm.'

'Thanks for rescuing me, by the way.'

'You were letting the draught in. Go to the window. See what they do now.'

Elsie moved to the window. There was no sign of the sisters.

'They've gone,' she said.

'Keep watching.'

Elsie did as he said and a moment later, the sisters emerged from somewhere behind the tower. Their baskets were heaped to the brim with firewood. Moving surprisingly quickly, they scuttled off into the trees, tails swishing.

'See?' said Corbett. 'Never leave empty-handed. Take anything that's not nailed down. Now listen.'

'For what?'

'Just listen.'

From somewhere in the distance, there arose two sudden, spine-chilling howls, sounding like hungry wolves on a winter's night.

'Goodness!' said Elsie. 'Is that them?'

'Yep,' said Corbett. 'Celebrating their swag.'

Elsie was just about to sit back down when there came a timid knock at the door.

'Parrot piddle!' sighed Corbett. 'What now?'

This time when Elsie opened the door she was faced with a slightly large girl who wore a flowing green gown. Frizzy brown hair hung down her back. Unwisely, she'd added a tiara of daisies. In her plump, pink arms was a resentful-looking white rabbit.

Ah. Aggie Wiggins, who dresses like a wood sprite, thought Elsie. *It has to be.*

Nuisance eyed the rabbit with interest but stayed where he was, clearly deciding against action. He had been promised cheese later. You didn't have to chase cheese.

'Hello,' said Elsie. 'Can I help you?'

'Oh,' said the girl. 'Isn't Miss Magenta in?'

'She's away. I'm Elsie, the caretaker.'

'I was wondering . . . is Hank coming today, by any chance?'

'I don't think so,' said Elsie. 'Magenta said he would be here tomorrow.'

The girl's face crumpled.

'Yes, but I thought – I hoped – oh, it doesn't matter. *Stop* it, Muffin!'

The rabbit was kicking and struggling to get away.

Elsie reached out to stroke the rabbit. It scrabbled crazily and made a lunge for freedom over the girl's shoulder. One of its legs became tangled in her ridiculous hair, causing the daisy chain tiara to slip over one eye, giving her a rather piratical look.

'Stand still,' said Elsie. 'Let me untangle you.' She reached up, unhitched the leg and straightened the daisies. 'There. That's better.'

'Thank you,' said the girl miserably. 'I'm Sylphine Greenmantle.'

'Nice to meet you, Sylphine,' said Elsie.

'When is she back? Miss Magenta?'

'In a week.'

'But she said . . . oh, never mind.'

Abruptly, she wheeled away. But Nuisance was in the way, as usual, and she tripped over him, falling clumsily on her hands and knees.

The rabbit shot off into the bushes. With a sob, Sylphine picked herself up and stumbled after it.

'What was that about?' Elsie asked Corbett as she returned again to the kitchen.

'She's got a crush on the woodcutter,' said Corbett. He gave a little smirk. 'Wants a love potion, but we're waiting for the ingredients to arrive. Takes time to arrive, time to make, time to ferment. You can't hurry love. That's a line from a song.'

'Corbett,' said Elsie, 'you really know a lot, don't you?' (Customer Service Rule Ten: Use Flattery. When people feel good about themselves, they buy more.)

'Well,' said Corbett, puffing out his chest, 'I do have years of useful knowledge. You could call it a bird's-eye view.'

'Exactly. I can learn a lot from you.' Elsie unhooked the bunch of keys. 'I bet you know this tower like the back of your hand. I mean wing. How do you fancy showing me round?'

'Well, it's getting close to my lunchtime . . .'

'You would be doing me an enormous favour. Just a lightning tour.'

'W-e-l-l . . .'

'Oh, thank you! You're a real darling! Where shall we start – top or bottom? You choose.'

Grumpy ravens are no different to difficult customers, Elsie thought to herself with a smile.

Chapter Seven
EXPLORING THE TOWER

They began at the top. Elsie stepped through a small door into a breezy world of green treetops and blue sky. Above, the red flag fluttered on its pole. Sticking out over the parapet was a long brass tube mounted on a tripod.

'That's the Spelloscope,' said Corbett, who was sitting on her shoulder. 'It's like a telescope, but with added functions.' His claws were digging into her a bit, but Elsie didn't want to complain now she was winning him over.

She stooped and applied one eye to the tube.

Corbett snatched a passing bug out of the air, swallowed and choked a bit. 'Ugh. That's one to avoid. What do you see?'

'Treetops and sky.'

'If you press the red button on the side it turns the magic on; then it'll home in on anyone you like. Just say their name.'

'What, this one?' Elsie put her finger on the red button.

'Not now!' Corbett held up a warning claw. 'Save it for later. Once you start, it's hard to stop. Let's keep moving. Lousy bugs up here.'

They descended the winding stone steps to the next level, where there was a red-painted door with a round brass knob.

'The office,' said Corbett. 'Shocking tip, since Magenta started **Sharp Spells on Tap**. You

need the key with the red ribbon.'

Elsie inserted the key in the lock. The door swung open with a squeal.

Corbett was right about the state of the room. It looked like a garage sale. Sagging shelves lined the walls, bearing hundreds of books. A lot of them were jammed in upside down and backward. Quite a few had fallen to the floor. A lopsided pegboard was plastered with yellowing scraps of paper bearing faded addresses, letters of complaint and lists of things to do.

Almost all of the floor was taken up with unravelling rolls of brown paper and mountains of cardboard boxes ranging from small to enormous. Set in the middle was a chaotic desk piled high with papers, scissors, balls of string, dried inkpots, old quill pens and dirty mugs. A dusty crystal ball was balanced precariously on top. The desk chair lay on its side, as

though its occupant had been unable to take the mess any longer and suddenly shot up and ran out, screaming.

But Elsie's eyes were on the shelves that lined the walls.

'The books!' she breathed. 'Just look at all those books!'

'Look at them later.' Corbett was getting fidgety. 'Come on, let's go, I haven't got all day.'

With a last lingering look, Elsie stepped out of the room, locking the door behind her. Down they went, to the next level.

'Her bedroom,' said Corbett, as they halted before a plain oak door. 'The purple ribbon. Not much to see.'

He was right. The room contained a bed with a plain grey coverlet, a wardrobe and a chest of drawers. Nothing else. Clearly Magenta's chaotic side was confined to the office.

Next to Magenta's room was a simple blue door – Elsie's favourite colour – and she assumed this must be where she would sleep. It was the only one left. It had to be.

'That's enough for now,' Corbett said. 'Let's go down to the kitchen, I'm busting for bugs. You hungry?'

Eager though Elsie was to inspect her bedroom, now that Corbett had mentioned food, she realized that she was starving. All she'd had that day was a bite of apple and a mouthful of milk.

Together, they went down the last flight of stairs. Elsie opened the front door, and Corbett flapped away over the trees in search of his lunch. Nuisance was still sitting on the doorstep, looking hopeful.

She went to the larder and cut herself a hunk of cheese and two thick slices of bread. She arranged it all on a plate with a big tomato and set it on the table. She then took a second plate and laid out the same for Nuisance.

'Here,' she said, taking it out and setting it down on the step. 'For you.'

In an instant, the dog was diving in.

The food was delicious, but Elsie felt strange to be eating at a table on her own, with only the ticking clock for company. Mealtimes at home were noisy, messy occasions. There was rarely much to eat, but there was always plenty of fun. She finished with a slice of cake (scrumptious), then collected Nuisance's empty plate and washed up. Nuisance was fast asleep on the step. Corbett was nowhere to be seen.

Elsie couldn't wait any longer. So, snatching

the bunch of keys, she ran up the first flight of steps to the blue door. She found a key with a blue ribbon and turned it in the lock. The door swung open.

'Oh…' breathed Elsie as she took in the room.

It was everything she had ever dreamed of. Pale blue walls and ceiling. Blue shutters over the window. A bed with a blue coverlet, patterned with tiny white clouds. A bedside table on which sat a single candlestick. A tiny chest of drawers, and a wardrobe – painted white, with blue handles. A wicker easy chair with a blue cushion. And an empty bookshelf. Waiting to be filled.

Elsie stepped in, closing the door behind her. Her room. Just hers.

There was a picture over the bed. She recognized it straight away. It was Pickles'

Emporium. Not as it was, but as it should be. How it could be, if money wasn't so tight. The windows weren't cracked, there was a fresh coat of paint on the door and the sign had all its letters. There was no sign of her family. Perhaps they were inside, eating turkey.

Feeling just a little bit homesick, Elsie turned away.

To distract herself, she opened the wardrobe. To her delight, it contained two crisp new cotton dresses – one blue with a white collar, the other a cheerful yellow. Yellow was her next best colour, after blue. She knew right away that they would fit her. On the bottom shelf was a pair of new leather boots.

She was tempted to try everything on, but first she had to try the bed. Eagerly, she kicked off her old boots, folded back the coverlet and stretched out.

It was like lying on a cloud. Her head sank into the fluffy pillows. The clean white sheet felt cool beneath her sore, scratched legs.

There was so much more to explore, but first, she would just lie there for a little while.

Just a little while . . .

Chapter Eight
MORE VISITORS

Elsie awoke to the sound of chopping. The moment she opened her eyes, she realized what she had done. She had slept through the rest of yesterday and the night – and now it was morning!

She'd never *ever* slept that long. It had to have been the bed. She jumped up, ran to the window and threw open the shutters.

Below, a broad-shouldered muscular boy was attacking a large branch with an axe – which explained the chopping noise. The boy wore a black vest and leather trousers. His long blond hair was tied back in a ponytail. Nuisance sat at a safe distance from the flying woodchips, ears alert, giving the occasional woof, enjoying all the noise and action.

'Slept all right, then,' said Corbett, as Elsie rushed down the stairs and hurried into the kitchen. 'You forgot to lock up last night. Some caretaker you are.'

'I'm sorry. I didn't mean to sleep for that long! I think it was the bed . . .'

Corbett sniffed. 'The Howlers came back in the night.'

'Oh no! Did they steal anything?'

'Your dog saw them off, so all they took was the bucket from the privy. They can never resist a bucket. We keep spares.'

Elsie felt guilty. Her first important task as caretaker and she'd failed. Thankfully, Nuisance had saved her bacon. She would reward him with an especially nice breakfast.

She was about to turn on the tap for a quick wash when the boy from the garden appeared in the archway, axe in hand. Up close, he had small eyes and a chin as wide as his neck.

'Hey?' he said, staring at Elsie with an air of

vague surprise. He set down the axe, took the band off his ponytail and shook out his yellow locks.

'Hello,' said Elsie. 'You must be Hank. I'm Elsie; I'm looking after the tower for a few days.'

'Yeah?' said Hank, swishing his hair, giving it a good airing. 'Hey.'

Elsie went to the change jar. Hank lounged against the wall, took a comb and a small mirror from his pocket and began combing. He did it with dedication. It was clearly something he loved to do.

'Here,' said Elsie, holding out the coins.

'Yeah, right, hey, cool, cheers.'

'Yeah,' said Elsie. 'Cheers.'

It was catching, this way of talking.

Hank gave a satisfied look at his reflection, pocketed the comb, the mirror and the money, shouldered his axe and strolled out.

Elsie was about to shut the door when Sylphine Greenmantle suddenly emerged from the trees. She wore the same gown as yesterday but had replaced the daisy chain with a bunch of bedraggled flowers behind one ear. Instead of Muffin the rabbit, today she was dragging a small, wild-eyed fawn on a length of green ribbon. It looked about as keen as Muffin had.

'Hello, Hank,' said Sylphine shyly, stepping into his path. 'I like your hair.'

Hank said not a word. Not even 'Hey'. He just brushed straight past her and swaggered off into the trees.

Sylphine went scarlet. The ribbon slipped from her fingers and the fawn bolted into the forest. Sylphine let it go. She stood radiating misery, like the last wood sprite to be chosen for the netball team.

'Sylphine?' called Elsie, taking pity. 'Would you like to come in and have a cup of tea?'

'You'll be sorry,' warned Corbett, from the kitchen. 'She'll cry.'

'She won't,' said Elsie. 'Not if there's cake.'

Ten minutes later, Sylphine was sitting at the kitchen table, weeping into her tea and telling Elsie her whole sorry story, in between mouthfuls of cake.

'. . . and I always wear my nicest dress (*sniff*)

and spend ages on my hair and everything and he doesn't even notice and I can't help having freckles or going blotchy when I'm nervous and he's always like that (*sniff, sniff*), he never says a single word to me even when I tell him I like his hair. Which I do. (*Sniff.*)'

'Is that all you like about him?' asked Elsie. 'His hair?'

'No. Yes. Mostly. I don't know.' Sylphine burst into fresh sobs.

'There, there,' said Elsie. 'More cake?'

'Yes, please. And the other woodcutters think it's funny. They're really mean and they laughed when they saw me dancing barefoot in the glade and the Howler Sisters stole my shoes – they're mean to me too. They sneak into my garden at night and empty the bird feeders and open the rabbit hutch.'

'You danced barefoot in a *glade?*' Elsie glanced down at Sylphine's large feet, which were currently clad in weird green moccasins.

'Yes. In the moonlight. I often do. I love dancing. It's how I express myself.'

From the perch, there came a little snort. Elsie caught Corbett's eye. He had clearly seen Sylphine's moonlight dancing and wasn't impressed.

'Why?' went on Sylphine, raising her pink eyes to Elsie. 'Do you think I shouldn't?'

'No, no . . . What sort of dancing?'

'It doesn't have a name. I don't need music. I just dance what I feel.'

'Mmm,' said Elsie, 'right. Er – what do you feel?'

'Miserable, mostly, because Hank won't speak to me.'

'Oh dear. More tea?'

'Yes, please (*sniff*). Have you got another hanky? This one's soaking.' Sylphine blew her nose noisily. 'And now Miss Magenta's gone away and she promised me a love potion. To make Hank like me. Corbett heard her, didn't you, Corbett?'

'Yes,' admitted the raven. 'If I recall correctly, her actual words were, "*All right, all right, I'll make your wretched potion, just go away, I've got bottles to wrap.*"'

Elsie thought that sounded like the witch.

'I expect she's waiting for the ingredients,' Elsie said, trying to make Sylphine feel better. 'Perhaps they're being slow to arrive.'

It must have been magic. No sooner had she said those words than a voice called from the front door.

'Hello? Anyone in? Make way, delivery coming through.'

A mop-headed boy with a sack over one shoulder came staggering in. Elsie and Sylphine jumped up and moved chairs out of his way as he hurried past and dumped a large cardboard box in the sink.

'Phew!' he said, standing

back. 'Glad to put that down. How's it going, Corbs? All right, Aggie?'

'Morning, Joey,' said Corbett. He held up a claw and the boy smacked it with an open palm.

'It's *Sylphine*,' said Sylphine. 'I keep telling you.'

'Oh, yeah, right, sorry, Ags, I keep forgetting.' The boy turned to Elsie. 'Who's this, then?'

'I'm Elsie,' she said. 'The caretaker. And you are?'

'Joey the post boy, happy to meet you. Away, is she? Her Witchiness?'

'Yes. Visiting her sister.'

'That won't go well.' He reached into his sack and took out a bundle of letters. 'Complaints. I'll stick 'em in the drawer with the others. Any of that cake going?'

Elsie cut him a big slice. She liked his open

face and his cheery grin. She saw Sylphine looking hopeful and cut her another one too.

Joey stuffed the bundle of letters into a drawer, which was already brimming over with others just like it. He leaned against Corbett's perch and took a huge bite of cake.

'Best open that quick,' he said, nodding at the box in the sink. 'Been stuck in the depot for weeks. Got dumped in a dark corner and forgotten about. It's making weird noises and releasing little pink hearts that smell like strawberries.'

Sylphine sat up, cake halfway to her mouth.

'It's them!' she squealed excitedly. 'The ingredients! Can we open it? Can we?'

Corbett had flown to the box and was examining the label.

WARNING!
Magical CONTENTS!
OPEN AND USE IMMEDIATELY!

'"**WARNING!**"' he read. '"**MAGICAL CONTENTS! OPEN AND USE IMMEDIATELY!**"'

Everyone stared at the box, which gave a jerk, right on cue. The lid rattled furiously. From inside, there came the sound of fizzing and popping. Whatever was in there had clearly had enough of being stuck in a box.

'I'll open it,' said Joey, finishing his cake. 'Got the tools, got the training. Always do the dodgy ones, don't I, Corbs?'

'He does,' said Corbett. 'He's very good.'

Joey took out a small pocketknife. 'Any idea what we're dealing with? Before I start?'

'If Sylphine's right, then it's ingredients for a love potion,' said Elsie.

'Yeah? Who's that for then, Aggie?'

'None of your business,' said Sylphine crossly. 'And it's *Sylphine*.'

'Off you go, then, Joey,' said Elsie. 'Do your thing.'

'Right,' he said. 'Stand back.'

He sliced neatly through the cardboard and pushed back the flaps.

'Hhhhhaaahhhhhhhhh . . .'

From out of the box came a long, whispering sigh of relief. It was the united sigh of tightly packed magical ingredients coming up for air.

'A load of bottles,' said Joey, poking around. 'And little packages and jars. Whoops!' He ducked as a stream of heart-shaped bubbles popped out and floated up in a pink cloud. The scent of strawberries filled the room. 'There they go! Lid's loose.'

He took out a large glass jar containing a bubbling pink mass and screwed the lid down properly.

The girls moved forward and curiously examined the tiny jars, oddly shaped bottles, small boxes and squishy packages as Joey emptied the box and laid the contents out on the draining board. Each was clearly labelled.

'"*Raindrops on Roses*",' read Sylphine. '"*Essence of Honeysuckle. Moon Mist. Pixie Mix*". Ooh! Doesn't it all sound lovely?'

Elsie picked up the jar of pink bubbles.

'"*Love Hearts*",' she read. The jar jerked in her hands and she hastily put it down. 'Gosh, they're lively.'

'"*Dried Sugar Candy*",' breathed Sylphine. '"*Rainbow Dust. All-Things-Nice Spice. Mermaid's Dream*".'

'"*Mermaid's Dream*"? Let me see that.' Elsie looked where Sylphine pointed. 'Looks empty to me.'

'What do you expect, cod and chips?' said Corbett.

When Joey had finished, a host of packages, jars, tins and tiny bottles cluttered the draining board. Some were still fizzing and popping.

'Well,' said Elsie, 'I suppose I'll have to find room in a cupboard.'

'But can't you start making the potion now?' asked Sylphine.

Elsie stared at her. '*I* can't make it. I'm not a witch.'

'But the label says "Use Immediately".'

Elsie shook her head. 'I'm just the caretaker. Spells and magic are not in the deal.'

'How hard can it be?' Sylphine wailed. 'All you have to do is follow a recipe!'

'I haven't got a recipe.'

'Yes, you have,' said Corbett. 'Top shelf on the right. *Everyday Recipes for the Practical Witch*. Love Potion. Page ninety-two.'

'Corbett,' said Elsie, 'whose side are you on? I've had no time to myself since I woke up. I haven't washed, unpacked, or cleaned my teeth. I haven't had breakfast or fed Nuisance. I haven't even *opened* a book. Nothing you or anyone can say will make me mess about with magic. And that's my final word.'

Chapter Nine
LOVE POTION

'How many Raindrops on Roses did you say?'

'Three heaped tablespoons,' said Corbett.

Moonlight streamed through the kitchen window. Elsie stood over the simmering cauldron, measuring out ingredients. Corbett perched on the table, reading out instructions from a large tattered book.

Elsie hadn't intended to do it. She had held out for ages, even when Sylphine had run off in floods of tears. Even when Joey had offered to return at the end of his round and help. Even when Corbett had warned her that 'Use Immediately' usually meant use immediately. She had washed, visited the privy, and made herself and Nuisance some late breakfast, all the while ignoring the ingredients for the potion, which stood in a great, hopeful cluster by the sink. Finally, she had sat down and opened *Everything You Need to Know*. This was the first chance she'd had to look at it and she was deeply curious.

There was only one page. One single white page.

Which was blank.

Elsie shut the cover. Again, the book seemed thick. She opened it again. Just the one page . . . What was going on?

'Put your thumb on it,' said Corbett.

'What?'

'Press your thumb on the page and say what's on your mind.'

Feeling rather silly, Elsie put her thumb on the page and said: 'Erm . . . we seem to have run out of cake?'

To her amazement, the page was suddenly filled with large black capitals.

TO ORDER FOOD ITEMS, KNOCK THREE TIMES ON THE LARDER STATING YOUR REQUIREMENT. THE TOWER WILL PROVIDE SAID ITEMS IMMEDIATELY. REMEMBER TO SAY PLEASE AND THANK YOU.

'Oh, my,' said Elsie. 'How useful.'

She walked to the larder door and rapped three times.

'Right. Ahem. Excuse me? Tower, could we have another cake, please?'

When she opened the door, a large cake sat on the middle shelf. Chocolate this time, with cherries on top. It had worked! This was magic she approved of.

She thanked the tower and thought she got a faint, friendly little quiver of acknowledgement in return.

The love potion ingredients were still there, though. Lurking in the corner. Spoiling her day. It felt like having lots of accusing eyes boring into her back.

Elsie threw a towel over them.

She spent the entire afternoon outside, trying to make Nuisance look less like a bush and more like a dog. She found a comb in a drawer and gently combed out his tangles. Corbett

condescended to help by picking out burrs and twigs with his beak. Nuisance had borne it bravely, only giving the occasional yelp when it all got too much.

Then Elsie had discovered an old tin tub hanging on a nail in the privy. So she lit the fire, boiled up six cauldrons of water, took some soap and a towel from the kitchen, picked Nuisance up and plonked him in.

He loved it! He splashed about happily for a good hour, and licked Elsie's face in gratitude when she finally hoisted him out and wrapped him in the towel. Underneath all the filth, he was quite handsome!

But he wouldn't come indoors. He just flopped on the doorstep, resting his head on his newly washed paws. Elsie sat down next to him for a while, watching the bats fly and enjoying the peace. Corbett perched on her shoulder, snapping at mosquitoes and shouting rude remarks to owls.

The light was fading when she finally went back inside. The towel she'd used to cover the ingredients was on the floor. Several of the jars on the draining board had popped their lids. Angry fizzing noises were coming from the bottles. The bag of Pixie Mix had exploded, showering the sink with purplish dust. More pink hearts were oozing from their jar.

'You've got to do it,' said Corbett urgently. 'Right now. Everything's unstable.'

'But it's getting late! It's almost dark outside.'

'Magic works best at night. Come on. I'll give you a claw.'

And that's how Elsie ended up in the candlelit kitchen, doing what she'd insisted she would never do. Messing about with magic.

A rosy fire glowed beneath the cauldron, which was giving off a delicious, sugary smell. The potion itself was rainbow coloured. Every time a new ingredient was added, it changed. Little pink hearts bubbled up from the surface and bobbed merrily about the rafters, catching the candlelight.

'What next?' asked Elsie.

'Ten drops of Moon Mist.'

'Right. Done. That's Raindrops on Roses,

Honeysuckle, Mermaid's Dream, Sugar Candy, Rainbow Dust, All-Things-Nice Spice and the rest of those perishing Love Hearts. Anything else?'

'A Maiden's Tears.'

Elsie examined the bottles. 'I don't see those.'

'They don't come in bottles. You'll need Sylphine's own silly tears. Here, use this.'

Corbett flapped to the table and picked up a sodden hanky with his beak.

'She blew her nose on that,' said Elsie. 'It's all snotty.'

'Plenty of tears there, though.'

'But won't it spoil it, having snot in?'

'Who cares? We won't be drinking it.' Corbett flapped to the cauldron and dropped it in. 'There. It'll all come out in the wash.'

'That's it? Are we done?'

'That's it. Just let it simmer. Tomorrow, when it's cold, pour it into the bucket under the sink and leave it to ferment.'

'How long for?'

'The recipe says three days.'

'Excellent!' said Elsie.

She could forget about it for three whole days. She had paid Hank. She had sorted out Nuisance. She had given out tea, cake and sympathy to Sylphine. She had ordered another cake. She had even written a note to her mum and dad to let them know she was okay, which Joey had promised to deliver.

Which meant that now she would have some time to herself.

The bookshelf in her bedroom was still empty. Tomorrow, perhaps, everyone would leave her alone so that she could finally sit down and read.

Chapter Ten
THREE WONDERFUL DAYS

The next three days were wonderful.

Elsie spent the first morning in Magenta's office. She brought up a huge bundle of complaining letters from the kitchen drawer and placed them carefully on the cluttered desk. Then she backed away on tiptoe, for fear of causing a landslide. Next, she turned her attention to the crowded shelves of books.

There were so many to choose from. Some were in different languages. Some were full of weird diagrams. Most were falling apart. There were old books of fairy stories, with strange pictures, which were tempting. But Elsie was looking for something different. Something interesting. The sort of book they didn't stock in the Smallbridge library.

Her eyes kept falling on a small book entitled *Three Little Spells for Beginners*.

No, she thought to herself. *Don't get sucked in. You've already made a love potion against your better judgement. Leave it at that.*

Firmly, she moved on past.

Ten minutes later, she went back again and took it from the shelf.

'Baby stuff,' scoffed Corbett, when she showed him. 'Anyway, I thought you wanted nothing to do with magic.'

'I don't,' said Elsie. 'I was just a bit curious.

I'll put it back and find something else.'

But she didn't.

She took the book into her bedroom, sat on her bed and began to read.

The first spell was making an egg appear from thin air. Carefully, she read the instructions. Apparently, it was just a matter of moving your fingers in a certain way, crossing your left leg over your right one and chanting a simple rhyme.

**OVER THE LEG,
GIVE ME AN EGG!**

A brown speckled egg materialized in the air and plopped gently into her lap. Simple!

Encouraged, Elsie practised making more eggs appear. The more she tried, the better she got, and soon she found she could order them singly or in a shower. She could even have them hard-boiled if she liked. It was just a matter of extra finger twiddles and small adjustments to the rhyme.

CROSS MY LUCKY LEGS,
GIVE ME HARD-BOILED EGGS!

Down they came out of nowhere, plopping onto her bed and rolling around the floor. When there were eggs everywhere and it all got a bit silly, she found she could make them disappear with a snap of the fingers and saying the rhyme backward.

SSORC YM YKCUL SGEL.
EVIG EM DRAH-DELIOB SGGE!

Nothing to it.

She felt absurdly pleased with herself. What was it Magenta had said about having the knack for magic?

She saved one of the eggs and ate it for lunch, along with a piece of chocolate cake.

She wanted to show the spell to Corbett, but he'd gone for a walk with Nuisance.

After lunch, she investigated the Spelloscope on the roof terrace. Just like Corbett had told her, when the magic button was pressed you could see whomever you liked. But not only that, you could hear what they were saying! Elsie spent the whole afternoon curiously observing her new neighbours.

First she zoomed in on the woodcutters' camp and watched Hank lounging in a hammock seeing to his hair while the other woodcutters

did all the work – cooking, sharpening their axes and washing their socks in a wooden tub. Their names, Elsie learned, were Ed, Ted, Fred, Jed, Ned and Short Shawn. All of them were muscular, as woodsmen should be, but none of them were as muscular as Hank, who they clearly held in great awe. They brought him chicken drumsticks, asked if he wanted a cushion, or a drink, or anyone to hold the mirror. They even helped dry his hair, which he apparently washed on a daily basis. Elsie knew this because there was a chart hanging on a tree headed HARE ROTER with a list of days and names. Hanging from the same tree was a fluffy towel and a bottle of special shampoo with Hank's name on.

Next Elsie spied on Sylphine, who lived in a tiny untidy cottage with a thatched roof.

Somebody must have told her that, as well as wearing weird, wafty dresses and dancing barefoot under the moon, wood sprites were known for having hordes of adoring animals following them everywhere. Consequently, her garden was full of stuff designed to tempt in the local wildlife. Bird feeders, hedgehog hotels, bird baths, a small pond, and lots of little notices everywhere reading: COME IN, ALL WELCOME, DEER SCRATCHING POST, SQUIRREL SANCTUARY, FOXES DRINK HERE! and suchlike. Sadly, whilst the local wildlife was happy to make use of the facilities, adoring Sylphine wasn't on the agenda. They ate the food provided, scratched on the post, bathed and drank their fill whenever Sylphine was asleep or out. Whenever she made an appearance, they all flapped, galloped, loped

or melted away just in case they were unlucky enough to get caught by her and taken on as her latest 'pet'.

Thankfully, Elsie didn't see Sylphine dancing barefoot in a glade. She was clearly too depressed about Hank.

Elsie tried spying on the Howler Sisters, but it didn't work. All she got was a view of the full moon in the night sky, although it was still broad daylight. It seemed that where and how the Howlers lived was a mystery.

When she tried getting through to the Emporium, the tower gave a disapproving little shiver and the Spelloscope refused to show anything but trees and sky. It was as though the magic had run out.

She asked Corbett about it as she sat down to eat her tea.

'Against the Ancient Rules,' he explained. '*Never try too far to see. What will be is what will be.*'

'That's a terrible rhyme,' said Elsie, 'but I suppose it makes sense. Whatever's happening at home, I can't do anything about it. Right, Tower?'

She waited for a little tremor of agreement, which didn't come. Maybe it didn't like its rhyme being criticized.

After she had finished tea, washed up and watered and fed Corbett and Nuisance, Elsie put *Everything You Need to Know* on the kitchen table, keen to ask it some more questions. She spent a long time pressing her thumb on the blank white page, asking questions and enjoying the novelty of seeing the answers swim into view.

Practical things like:
'Where do I put the rubbish?'

BACK OF THE PRIVY BY THE WOODPILE.

Interesting things like:
'Does the tower really have an ancient rule about ravens never doing the washing up?'

NO. HE'S LYING.

Silly things like:
'Are there fairies at the bottom of the garden?'

DON'T WASTE MY TIME.

She asked what to do in an emergency. The words came up:

CONTACT ME ON THE CRYSTAL BALL IN THE OFFICE.

She read this out to Corbett.

'Did she give the password?' he asked.

'Password? No.'

'Pointless, then. You'll just have to cope if there's a problem. Lucky you've got me.'

'It is,' said Elsie. And it was. Grumpy though he was, she enjoyed Corbett's company. It was nice to have someone to chat to. Because as much as she was enjoying life at the tower, she found she was missing her family and all the hustle and bustle that came from living on top of each other. Despite his healthy worm-and-bug diet, she found that Corbett was partial to cake. Between them, they got through a lot of it.

When she went to bed, she discovered her bedroom drawers now contained a brush and comb, and blue and yellow ribbons for her hair. There was also a blue nightgown, decorated with little yellow moons. Plus a hand mirror that made her look better than usual.

That night, she dreamed of skipping over sunlit hills in blue dancing shoes, and cleverly juggling eggs.

Outside in the forest, the moon sailed high over the trees. Nuisance, fast asleep on the doorstep, snuffled happily in his sleep.

Under the kitchen sink, the potion fermented.

★ ★ ★ ★

On the second morning, Elsie put on one of the new dresses Magenta had left for her – it fitted perfectly, as she had known it would – and changed into the new boots. Feeling the need for some fresh air, after breakfast, she carefully locked all the rooms, double locked the front door and took Nuisance for a long walk. Corbett came along too, riding on her shoulder and shouting insults at wood pigeons. This time, Elsie did pick some bluebells. The forest didn't seem so threatening any more. Once you lived somewhere, you began to see its nice side. She was beginning to feel she belonged.

She spent most of the afternoon in her room with *Three Little Spells for Beginners*. She

produced some more eggs from
the air. No trouble. Eggs were
easy.

Elsie moved on to spell two.
A storm in a teacup.

After a few failures (hurrying too
much and getting the finger shapes wrong) she
managed to produce a perfect little storm, with
tiny flashes of lightning and sweet little rumbles
of thunder. A small rain cloud hovered above the
cup's rim. The tea splashed about, like a miniature
brown sea.

She learned that if you added sugar, you could
make it hail!

Next, she worked on making the storm come
out of the cup. The instructions were to throw
your arms up, move your fingers a certain way
and say:

UP, UP! OUT OF THE CUP!

With a slurping noise, the tiny black cloud sucked up the tea. It then shot up, massively increasing in size, boiling around the ceiling before unleashing a deluge of tepid brown liquid that instantly soaked Elsie's bed. The tiny lightning bolts merged into one massive one that stabbed down, leaving the wardrobe with a nasty charred mark. The accompanying clap of thunder nearly burst her eardrums in such a confined space. Down in the kitchen, Corbett fell off his perch. Elsie decided it was probably not a good idea to practise that one indoors.

She was pleased with herself, though. Could it really be that she was one of those people who had the knack? She asked Corbett.

'Well, obviously,' said Corbett, cleaning his

feathers with his beak. 'Why else do you think Magenta chose you?'

'She didn't *choose* me,' said Elsie. 'It just happened that way.'

'Hmm,' said Corbett.

★ ★ ★

Early that evening, the Howlers came to call. Elsie knew before they even arrived, because Nuisance, who still refused to come into the tower, started barking like crazy, going into fierce guard dog mode.

'Bald buzzards with knobs on, they're back,' sighed Corbett.

The two little figures – one blue, one pink – hovered at the edge of the glade.

'Hello, Elsie, dear,' called Ada, waving her parasol. 'Can you call your dog off?'

'We'd love to pop in, if it's convenient,'

called Evie.

'Sorry,' shouted Elsie. 'I'm a bit busy.' Firmly, she shut the door.

A moment later, two howls resounded throughout the treetops.

'That's another bucket gone from the privy, I reckon,' said Corbett, and he was right.

Shortly after that, Joey popped in with another bundle of complaints. He and Corbett did the usual claw/hand greeting, then Joey hopped onto the table.

'Phew. That's the round finished,' he sighed 'How's the caretaking going, Elsie?'

'Good,' replied Elsie.

'What have you been up to?'

'Reading, mostly. Learning how to do . . . things.'

'What "things"?'

'Well – spells and stuff.'

'I thought you weren't going to mess about with magic,' he said trying to hide a smile.

'I'm not,' said Elsie.

'*Ahem!*' said Corbett.

'Well – not much.'

'*Ahem!*'

'Well, all right, I can do two *little* spells. But they're easy.'

'You made the love potion, too, didn't you? I can smell it,' said Joey. 'You should have invited me. I did offer to help.'

'Corbett was here and it was quite straightforward really. Did you give my note to my mum and dad?'

'Of course. They said to tell you they've spent the pennies on a new bell. And they miss you.'

'I miss them too,' said Elsie. And she did. But

there was so much happening that she didn't miss them *too* much.

That night, Elsie dreamed of bustling around a crowded tea shop with a tray of teacups containing tiny storms. Everybody seemed very pleased with their storm and showered her with gold coins.

Under the sink, the potion fermented.

On the third day, Elsie felt pretty confident with eggs and small storms, so she moved on to the third spell from *Three Little Spells for Beginners*. A short time later, she could conjure up frogs! Sweet little green ones. She demonstrated to Corbett on the kitchen table. He looked at them with a glint in his eye, so she hastily made them vanish. But she knew she could make them come back again, any time.

She was getting good, she knew that. So much so that she didn't need the book any more. She knew all the rhymes and finger movements by heart.

That night, she dreamed that she was sitting on a large lily pad on a moonlit lake, watching a cast of little green frogs perform a water ballet. She was tempted to join them, but didn't want to get her blue shoes wet.

And under the sink, the potion still fermented . . .

Chapter Eleven
CAKE

'Have you checked the love potion?' asked Corbett. It was the morning of day six of Elsie's caretaking, and she was eating a boiled egg and idly conjuring up a small storm in her morning cup of tea. Three newly materialized little green frogs sat behind the pepper pot, keeping a close eye on Corbett. It was a warm day. A welcome breeze blew in the open window and out through the front door, which they'd left ajar.

'No,' said Elsie. 'Goodness. Have three days gone already?'

'Yep. It should be ready by now.'

Elsie pulled the bucket out from under the sink. Peering inside she saw a wobbly pink goo that looked a little like blancmange. It smelled of honey, flowers and strawberries.

'Morning,' said Joey, sticking his head through the window. He placed a foot on the sill and jumped into the room. 'It's my day off, so I came to see if the potion's ready. Is that it? Wow! Fantastic smell! Can I have a taste?'

'Not unless you want to fall in love with Sylphine,' replied Elsie.

'It's got her snot in it,' added Corbett.

'I'll give it a miss, then. Does Aggie know you made it?'

'It's *Sylphine,*' came a cross voice from the archway. 'How many more times?'

'Hello, Sylphine,' said Elsie. 'That's a nice

tortoise you've got in your hair.'

It was a sentence she never thought she'd say.

A small tortoise was indeed caught up in a long lock of Sylphine's frizzy hair, waving its little legs, clearly furious. Sylphine advanced into the kitchen, yanking at the poor animal none too gently.

'Stand still, you're making it worse,' said Elsie, and untangled it. She put the tortoise on the floor, where it immediately made for the door in a slow but determined escape bid.

'Thanks,' said Sylphine. 'Oswald and I were just passing, and we smelled this lovely, sugary— What's that in the bucket? Is it my love potion? Oh, Elsie! You made it!'

She threw her arms around Elsie,

nearly knocking her over.

'I did,' said Elsie, disentangling herself. 'Now all we have to do is get it down Hank's throat.'

'Hah!' cried Joey. 'So *that's* who you've got a crush on!'

'Shut up!' snapped Sylphine, going red.

The four of them stared into the bucket.

'It's not exactly a *potion*, is it?' said Joey. 'More . . . gloopy than runny.'

'He won't eat that,' said Corbett. 'Too sweet and too pink. No way.'

'He could use it as hair gel,' suggested Joey. 'On his lovely hair. Would that work?'

'No,' said Corbett. 'The recipe was very clear. It has to be taken by mouth.'

'Aggie will have to wrestle him to the floor and force-feed him with a spoon, then.'

'*Be quiet*, Joey,' said Sylphine. 'I don't think

that's funny. *And it's Sylphine.*'

'I'll try asking the book,' said Elsie. 'It might have a suggestion.'

'What book?' chorused Joey and Sylphine.

'Magenta left a sort of guide,' said Elsie, going to the table and opening *Everything You Need to Know*. 'It's got all kinds of useful information.'

Joey and Sylphine gazed at the single blank page.

'There's nothing there,' said Sylphine.

'Wait,' said Corbett. 'Watch.'

Everyone watched Elsie press her thumb on the page.

'Any suggestions on how we get Hank to drink love potion?'

A single word appeared in the centre of the page.

CAKE

'Brilliant!' cried Joey. 'Everyone likes cake.'

'Right,' said Elsie, reaching for her apron. 'I think a sponge is called for. You can't go wrong with a sponge.'

The cake was a masterpiece. A golden, perfectly risen sponge cake in two layers, with red jam in the middle. It looked like regular cake and it smelled like regular cake – perhaps a little bit sweeter. You would never guess that it contained love potion.

Elsie had done most of the work. She loved baking. Pickles' Emporium didn't bring in much money, but they always managed to scrape together enough to make a cake for special occasions.

The others had helped Elsie a bit, but mostly they just stood around getting under her feet while she measured, whisked and poured. When she found she had run out of eggs, instead of asking the tower, she conjured one out of the air without even thinking about it.

'Wow!' said Sylphine. 'You didn't say you could do that!'

'Elsie, you *are* a mini witch!' Joey said. 'Ladies and gents, for her next trick, fried snowballs!'

There was some discussion about how much fermented love potion to put in. All of it or just a teaspoon? In the end, Elsie added three heaped, wobbling tablespoons to the mix, because that felt about right. She had handed the wooden spoon to Sylphine and told her to give it a stir and make a wish. That felt right too.

So now here it was. A beautiful cake sitting on Magenta's best plate, all ready for the eating.

'It's wonderful!' cried Sylphine. 'Elsie, you are the best friend ever!' She clapped her hands, twirled on the spot and knocked over a chair.

'Thanks,' said Elsie with a smile. She really was getting the hang of magic now!

'Shame we can't try it,' said Joey. 'It's making me drool.'

'There's an apple pie in the larder,' said Elsie. 'We can have that instead. Off you go, Sylphine.'

'What? Where?' said Sylphine, looking alarmed.

'To the woodcutters' camp. I'm guessing that's where Hank is.'

'Now?'

'Yes. Why not? Strike while the cake's hot.'

'Oh,' said Sylphine. 'Yes, I suppose so.'

'You seem a bit unsure,' said Elsie. 'Have you changed your mind?'

'What? Oh, no. No, of course not. Um . . . what should I say?'

'Say: "Hello, Hank, here's a cake".'

'Which definitely doesn't have love potion in it,' added Joey.

'Or snot,' said Corbett. They both sniggered.

'Should I tell him his hair looks nice?' asked Sylphine.

'*No!*' chorused everyone.

'Let the cake do its job,' added Elsie. 'First, Hank will eat it. Then you can talk about his hair. One bite of this and you should be able to tell him his hair looks like a haystack in a gale and he'll still think you're the bee's knees.'

'Yes. Right . . . um . . . I should go and change my dress first, though. And put some flowers in my hair. And I don't know where Oswald's got to, I really ought to—'

'Don't make excuses,' said Elsie. She picked up the plate containing the fragrant cake and placed it firmly in Sylphine's hands. 'Good luck. Go. Now.'

'Can't one of you come with me?'

'No. This has to be done by you.'

'But what if it doesn't work?'

'It'll work,' said Elsie. 'We read the instructions and followed the recipe.'

'All right,' said Sylphine. 'I'll try.'

'Make sure you invite us to the wedding,' said Corbett.

'Break a leg, Aggie,' said Joey. 'Actually, don't.'

The three of them went to the door and watched Sylphine walk off into the trees.

'She'll mess it up,' said Corbett. 'I've got that feeling.'

'She'll drop it,' said Joey. 'She's always tripping up over those droopy dresses she wears.'

'Be brave, Sylphine!' shouted Elsie, trying to be supportive. 'Have faith in the cake!'

Secretly, though, she was a bit worried. It was

only a guess as to how much potion to add. Was it too much? Too little? Suppose Hank turned down the cake, just to be mean? He seemed to get real pleasure out of being rotten to Sylphine.

'I wish we were flies on the wall,' said Joey. 'Then we could see what happens. Better still, birds in the tree. Learned any spells that can turn us into birds, Elsie?'

'Afraid not.' Elsie shook her head. 'I can only do eggs, frogs and storms in teacups.'

'I'm a bird already,' pointed out Corbett. 'I could fly over to the woodcutters' camp, see how it's going and report back.' He clapped a wing to his head. 'Wait a minute! No need. We've got the Spelloscope!'

'Of course!' cried Elsie.

The three of them turned as one and made for the stairs.

Which meant that nobody noticed as Nuisance emerged from under a bush, stretched, sniffed the air and then trotted off into the trees.

Chapter Twelve
THE WOODCUTTERS' CAMP

The woodcutters' camp was easy to find, if you knew your way around Crookfinger Forest. It helped that there was a wooden sign erected by the side of a narrow path. It bore a painted arrow and the words:

The camp took over the whole of a large clearing. In the middle was a fire with a big pot suspended above, in which bubbled some sort of brownish stew. To one side was a massive tree stump, with six axes stuck in it. Hank's hammock was currently unoccupied.

A rickety shed sat on one side of the glade. It was where the woodcutters slept when it was raining and it consisted of just two rooms. Hank had the largest one all to himself because he had the biggest muscles and the best hair. The small room housed Ed, Ted, Ned, Fred, Jed and Short Shawn.

Right now, Ed, Ted, Ned, Fred, Jed and Short Shawn were sitting round the fire in the centre of the clearing, engaged in a rowdy sing-song. Their rough voices rose in the air.

*'If yer 'appy and you knows it, choppa tree
(chop, chop!)*

*If yer 'appy and you knows it, choppa tree
(chop, chop!)*

If yer 'appy an' you . . . knows it—'

Suddenly, the singing dwindled away into silence as the woodcutters noticed Sylphine standing nervously on the edge of the glade, the cake in her hands.

'Well, well,' said Ed. 'We gotta visitor.'

'Aggie Wiggins, no less,' said Ted.

'What's that you got, Aggie?' said Ned. 'A cake, is it?'

'Is that fer us, Aggie?' said Jed.

'It's Sylphine,' said Sylphine. Her voice wobbled a bit. 'And the cake is for Hank.'

Slowly, all six woodcutters stood up, eyes on the cake.

'Hank ain't 'ere,' said Fred. 'Gone to the barber's.'

'You can leave it wiv us,' chipped in Ed. 'We'll see'e gets it.'

The six of them moved closer.

'No,' said Sylphine, trying to sound brave. 'I want to give it to him myself.'

'What's the matter, Aggie? Don't ya trust us?' said Ed. He held out a huge hand. ''And it over.'

'No,' quavered Sylphine, backing away.

Ed's shadow fell over her, and then something happened that nobody expected.

There came a blood-curdling snarl and Nuisance exploded from a nearby nettle patch! His teeth were bared and his fur stood on end. Elsie's frizzy-haired friend was being threatened and it was up to him to protect her! *Grrrr! Ark, ark! Woof!* All that! Whatever it took! To the rescue!

Sylphine wasn't expecting him. His sudden appearance startled her as much as the woodcutters and she screamed and lurched backwards, catching her heel in her hem. The cake sailed from her hands and fell to the ground with a moist plop.

The woodcutters drew back in alarm, away from Nuisance's slavering jaws and demented barking.

Sylphine looked down at the ruined cake. It lay amongst the forest debris, deflated, covered with dirt and surrounded by broken pieces of plate.

'Now see!' she wailed. 'Oh, you – you – you *beasts*, you! You mean, horrible *boys*! Everything's spoiled!' With a muffled sob, she sped away into the forest.

Back at the tower, it was a despondent party that trailed down from the roof and into the kitchen.

'She blew it,' said Corbett. 'I knew she would. Clumsy as a one-legged chicken.'

'They would have taken it off her anyway,' said Joey. 'They're real mean, that lot. After all the trouble we went to, though. What a waste.'

'Oh, well.' Elsie gave a sigh. 'I'd better wash up, I suppose. The kitchen's a mess.'

'We'll help, won't we, Corbs?' Joey said, grabbing the bucket with the leftover love potion. 'I'll get rid of this. You can dry.'

'Eh? All right, if I must.' Reluctantly, Corbett

picked up a tea towel with his beak.

Gloomily, the three of them tidied up in silence.

A short time later, they sat at the table, staring down at a large apple pie. But none of them felt much like eating now.

There came a hammering at the door, and the sound of snivelling.

'It's her,' said Elsie. 'Be nice, both of you, all right? Joey, don't you dare call her Aggie.'

Elsie opened the door to a stricken-looking Sylphine. Her red face was streaked with tears.

'It didn't work!' she wailed.

'Come in, I'll find you a hanky,' said Elsie. Back in the Emporium, her dad kept a pile of clean hankies under the counter. (Customer Service Rule Nine was Always Have a Handy Hanky for Upset Customers).

'Hank wasn't even there but the others were and they tried to take it off me and they said they'd give it to him but they were lying and then that Nuisance dog jumped out and I tripped up and I *dropped* it!'

'I know. We saw.'

'What? How?'

'There's a thing called a Spelloscope at the top of the tower. We watched through that. Please don't cry. I'll make you a nice cup of tea.'

'Bad luck, Ag – Sylphine,' said Joey. 'Sorry it didn't work out.'

'Calm down,' said Corbett. 'Have some apple pie.'

'Oh, there's pie?' Sylphine perked up. 'Well, maybe just a small piece.'

'That's more like it,' said Elsie, cutting a big slice. 'Put the kettle on, Joey. I need to do something.'

She took a handful of dog biscuits from the larder, went back to the door and looked out.

'Nuisance?' she called. 'Are you there?'

There was a moment's pause, then the bushes parted and Nuisance's head poked out. He had

a peculiar look
on his whiskery
face. Pleased with
himself, but not sure
he should be. He'd done what
he thought was right, but the frizzy-haired
girl had confused him. All that shouting and
crying. Had he done something wrong? Was
he a bad dog?

He approached the step uncertainly.

'Good dog,' said Elsie. 'You did great. Here.'
She put the biscuits on the step.

But Nuisance didn't make a move to take
them. His ears were pricked and his fur was
rising. Sharply, he turned his head and snarled.

Ed, Ted, Ned, Fred, Jed and Short Shawn
were emerging from the trees. They stood
hovering at the edge of the glade.

Nuisance growled louder.

'Shush,' said Elsie. 'I'll handle it.' She raised her voice. 'Yes? Can I help you?' (Customer Service Rule Seven: Always Be Helpful.)

'We wants ter see Sylphine,' shouted Ed, who seemed to be clutching a droopy bunch of bluebells. 'We know she's in there!'

'Well, she doesn't want to see you!'

'But we wants to invite her for supper, tell'er! Stew! Wiv lumps!'

'She'll love it,' added Fred. 'I does.'

'She can 'ave the best bowl,' promised Ned. 'We'll wash it out!'

'Tell 'er we finks she's bootiful,' said Jed. '*Bootiful* as a . . . like a . . . I dunno, what's bootiful?'

'My granny's got a nice vase,' supplied Short Shawn helpfully. 'Yeller.'

'There yer go! Bootiful as Shawn's gran's vase!' cried Jed.

'Yeah,' agreed the others. 'She's lovely is Sylphine.'

'We wants 'er to be our girlfriend,' added Short Shawn.

Elsie looked down at Nuisance, who was waiting for orders.

'Guard the step. Keep them at bay, but no biting.' Firmly, she closed the door.

'What's up?' asked Joey, spooning tea into the pot. 'Somebody out there?'

'The woodcutters are here,' said Elsie. 'Bad news. I think they've eaten the cake.'

'Ah,' said Corbett. 'Complications. That can happen with spells.'

'But it fell on the ground,' said Sylphine, scraping pie off her plate. 'It was all dirty, with bits in it.'

'Well, they must have picked it up and eaten it anyway. Now they all really like you and want you to go to supper and eat brown stew with lumps in.'

'Well, they're out of luck,' said Sylphine. 'I don't want stew. What I really want is more pie. Is there any cream?'

From outside, there arose a sudden chant.

'*Sylphine, Sylphine! Come wiv us an' be our queen! Sylphine! Sylphine! Come wiv us an' be our queen!*'

'Ignore them,' said Elsie. 'They'll go away.'

'When, though?' asked Joey.

'I don't know. When the cake's out of their system?'

'Could be in for a long wait, then,' said Joey. 'Tomorrow morning, if we're lucky.'

'Sylpheeeeen!' came Ed's pleading voice. 'Come an' get yer luverly flowers wot we picked.'

Suddenly, a new voice broke in.

'Out of the way, young man, we're coming through. Sylphine, dear? Are you in there? Ada and I want to invite you to tea!'

'We think of you like a granddaughter, dear!' chimed in a second voice. 'Cucumber sandwiches and three sorts of jam! Do come.'

This was greeted by a hail of furious barking from Nuisance. *More enemies! See 'em off! Grrr! Ark!*

In the kitchen, everybody stared at each other.

'Joey,' said Elsie. 'When we cleared up, where did you put the rest of the love potion? That was in the bucket?'

'Put it out the back, next to the privy, so it was out of the way,' said Joey. 'Why? Oh, you don't think . . . ?'

'The Howler Sisters have got a thing about buckets,' said Elsie.

Outside, Sylphine's admirers were gearing up for a new onslaught.

'Stew!' shouted Short Shawn. 'Made wiv me own 'ands wot I washed day before yesterday!'

'I've rit you a pome, Sylphine!' bellowed Fred. 'Sylphine, you're the queen of 'earts, around you we won't do no f—'

'Sylphine, dear, come home with us and see the lovely shawl we knitted for you!' Evie begged.

'We want to adopt you, dear!' Ada trilled.

Ark! barked Nuisance, beside himself. *Ark! Ark! Grrrrr!*

'What a racket,' said Sylphine, poking around in the larder for cream. 'What should we do?'

'Put a stop to it,' said Elsie firmly. 'I've had enough. I'm all for good Customer Service, but some people just don't know when it's closing time. Come on, Corbett. Back me up.'

Chapter Thirteen
THREE LITTLE SPELLS

Corbett on her shoulder, Elsie wrenched open the front door and stepped out.

Nuisance stopped barking and shuffled over to make room. The woodcutters and the Howlers fell quiet. There was clearly to be some sort of announcement.

'Right,' said Elsie. 'Now, listen to me. All this nonsense has to stop. You don't really love Sylphine at all.'

'We do,' chorused the besotted woodcutters.

'Oh, but we *do!*'

'As for us, we think she's a delightful young lady,' said Ada. 'We *adore* her, don't we, Evie?'

'No, you don't,' said Elsie. 'You steal her shoes and vandalize her garden.'

'Oh, my! As if we would!' gasped Evie. 'Hear that, Ada? Such fibs!'

'Listen,' said Elsie. 'You're not yourselves. It's because of a love potion. It's your own fault. You either ate cake that wasn't meant for you or licked leftover pink goo out of a bucket.'

'Sho go away and leave me alone,' chipped in Sylphine indistinctly, coming up from behind with her mouth full of pie. 'The potion wash for Hank, and he'sh the only one who didn't have any. Mmm, thish pie ish *lovely.*'

'Oooh!' moaned the watching crowd, awash

with love. 'It's her!'

'I didn't have any potion,' said Joey, sticking his head around the door. 'It's got snot in it.'

Everyone went a bit quiet at that.

'Thank you, Sylphine. Thank you, Joey,' said Elsie. 'Everybody clear now? The potion was meant for Hank, not any of you. I'm sure the magic will wear off. Please go quietly home and—'

'Hey?' Another voice came from the shadows. 'Someone say my name, yeah?'

And a tall figure strolled into the glade.

It was Hank, back from the barber's with a truly radical haircut.

Someone – some creative, experimental hair artist, or maybe someone who just didn't like Hank – had ignored those all-important words: *Just a trim, yeah?*

Hank had been given a weird, thick fringe which hung over his eyes. The rest had been cut so short, he was bordering on bald. That same someone had left a silly little dangling pigtail trailing down his neck. It was one of those haircuts that haunt you for ever.

It was a haircut that screamed *Big Mistake!*

Even Hank wasn't too sure about his new look. It was certainly different. But was it cool?

The hairdresser had assured him that it was, but Hank wasn't convinced. Didn't it make his neck look too wide? His face too short? Was the pigtail a mistake? When he tried tossing his head, nothing happened. There was no familiar, reassuring swish. The swish had been left behind, along with the pile of shorn yellow locks on the shop floor.

Nobody had complimented him on his new look. In fact, the other customers had gone very quiet when he stood up to leave. Even the other barbers stopped snipping and stared. Only Hank's hairdresser seemed truly happy.

Oh, well. He would just brazen it out. Yeah, right. He was cool enough to carry it off. Wasn't he?

'Hey,' said Hank again. 'What's up, guys, yeah?'

The Howler Sisters whispered to each other behind their hands, looking outraged as only little old ladies can when presented with youths with strange and terrible hair.

Ed, Ted, Ned, Fred, Jed and Short Shawn stared, open-mouthed, too shocked to laugh. That would come later.

Sylphine went red. Then white. Then a normal colour. She folded her arms, shook her head and said, 'Oh. What was I thinking? That. Is. Truly. *Awful*.'

'Ah, Hank,' said Elsie. 'I was just telling everyone to go home.'

'We won't, though!' shouted Ed, brandishing his bluebells. 'Not wivout Sylphine. She's comin' fer supper!'

'Huh?' said Hank, startled. 'Aggie Wiggins? Why's *she* coming to supper?'

'Don't you call 'er that,' snarled Ted. 'She don't like it.'

'Yeah,' growled Ed, Fred, Ned, Jed and Short Shawn as one. 'You leave 'er alone.'

'She's our girlfriend,' added Ted. 'Show some respec' or we'll duff you up.'

'No need for violence, young man,' snapped Ada. She raised her parasol and rapped him smartly on the head.

'Not in the presence of a young lady,' added Evie. 'Come home with us, Sylphine, dear, this is no place for you!'

Hank and his alarming hair had been a distraction for a moment, but now Sylphine's fan club was back on track. Another chant was starting up. Nuisance began barking again.

'Corbett,' said Elsie. 'They're not listening. What shall we do?'

'You don't need me to tell you,' said Corbett. 'You've got new skills. Use 'em.'

'Right,' said Elsie. 'Eggs first. I know I can do those. Somebody fetch an umbrella.'

The eggs were a triumph. Elsie thought hard-boiled would have the most impact, and they came hurtling from the sky, bouncing painfully on heads and shoulders, then down to the ground, where they rolled around. In seconds, the forest floor was a sea of white. The Howlers squealed and put up their parasols. Arms over their heads, the woodcutters ran for the shelter of the trees, eggs crunching underfoot.

Sadly, it was an easy little spell, not designed to last, especially when delivered at maximum strength. So after a short, sharp egg shower, the magic ran out. The air cleared and the eggs on the ground melted away into thin air.

So did Hank. He'd had enough for one day. Silly hair, mutiny in the woodcutter ranks, everyone developing a mysterious passion for Aggie Wiggins and egg rain. It was time to

slink off home and look for a hat.

'Now, will you please go away?' called Elsie.

'Yeah!' shouted Corbett. 'Clear off!'

But Sylphine's devoted fans came creeping forward again. It was going to take more than an egging to shift them.

So Elsie did little green frogs.

A rain of frogs is worse than boiled eggs. Not so painful, but generally much more unpleasant, judging by the fuss everyone made. They plopped and hopped, those little frogs. They leapt and crawled over feet and down necks, croaking and flexing their cold, slimy, tiny limbs.

'Don't send 'em back, I'll have a few when this is over,' said Corbett.

But he was out of luck.

The spell ran out of steam, the frog rain eased off and they vanished of their own accord just like the eggs had done.

'*Now* will you go home?' shouted Elsie.

Sylphine's admirers were shaken, but still not inclined to stir. Sylphine herself was on her third slice of pie and was clearly starting to enjoy the attention.

'Right,' said Elsie. 'They asked for it. Joey, could I have a cup of tea?'

'Huh? What, now?'

'Now. Only a drop of milk. Six sugars.'

'Whooo-hoo!' crowed Corbett. 'Really?'

'Really,' said Elsie. 'I know what I'm doing. In fact, I'm looking forward to it.'

Eggs had been bad. Frogs had been worse. But Elsie's storm in a teacup was a sight to behold!

Released from the cup, free at last, it expanded! The tiny black cloud became a huge, billowing mass, rising above the treetops, growing up and outward until it filled the sky. The glade darkened. There was a pause. Then a bolt of lightning zapped down, setting a small bush on fire!

Then came the thunder. A terrible, strident crack, as though the sky was splitting in two.

'Get back!' shouted Elsie. 'It's tea time!'

Everyone moved back from the doorway. And then—

Then came the tea. Huge, heavy drops of scalding tea with hardly any space between them. There were hard grains of sugar mixed in, like hailstones. Branches

sagged, trees bent and
the ground became a
churned-up mass of mud.

Love has its limits, and for
Sylphine's admirers this was it. With one
accord, the mob in the glade took to their
heels.

'Wow!' said Joey, as the howls and
screams died away. 'That was *good*, Elsie.'

'Impressive,' said Corbett. 'I gotta claw
it to you.'

'How did you *do* that?' gasped Sylphine.
They all stood in the doorway, gazing out at
the gently steaming landscape.

'Practice,' said Elsie.

True, of course. But as we all know,
with magic it helps to have the knack.

Chapter Fourteen
HOME

The following morning, Elsie awoke to the smell of burning!

Instantly, she was out of bed and running down the stairs.

'Good morning,' said Magenta, as Elsie burst into the kitchen. 'I'm just making myself some breakfast.'

The witch was standing next to the stove, spreading butter on a piece of black toast. She still wore her travelling clothes. Her carpet bag was parked by the door, along with a large straw sunhat, a small cardboard box and a stuffed donkey. 'Oh!' gasped Elsie. 'You gave me a fright. How long have you been back?'

'Long enough to fall out with Corbett. He doesn't like the donkey I bought him as a gift. Flown off for a sulk. That dog of yours looks a whole lot better. Give him a bath, did you?'

'I did,' said Elsie.

'So,' said Magenta, flinging herself into the rocking chair and kicking off her shoes. 'How did you find being a caretaker? Any problems? I must say everything looks shipshape. Although I see someone set fire to a bush outside. And do I detect a faint smell of tea in the air?'

'Yes,' said Elsie. 'I, um . . . let loose a storm in a teacup. Yesterday. Bit of an emergency.'

'You handled it, though.'

'Yes. I've been – sort of *dabbling* with magic a bit.'

'Uh-huh. How did you get on?'

'Quite well,' said Elsie. 'I think I might have the knack.'

'Yes, I thought you might. Put the kettle on and you can tell me all about it.'

'All right,' said Elsie. 'Don't eat that burnt toast. I'll make you an omelette. I can do *really* good things with eggs.'

It was a long breakfast. There was a lot to tell. Magenta listened with great interest and nods of approval. When Elsie enquired about her holiday with her sister, she said, 'Don't ask.' So Elsie didn't.

After breakfast, Elsie packed her things, ready to go home. At Magenta's insistence, she took the new dresses, the ribbons, the brush

and comb home with her. When her basket was full, she took a last look around the blue bedroom. At the wonderful bed, where she had slept for seven blissful, undisturbed nights. At the blue bedspread, which still bore the stains of tea. At the charred mark on the wardrobe. At the one book on the shelf. *Three Little Spells for beginners,* which in the end had been all she'd had time to read. Magenta had invited her to take the book home, but Elsie declined. Her little brothers would only chew it.

She was sad to leave. After so much fun and excitement, life in Smallbridge would seem more boring than ever.

She glanced briefly at the painting of the Emporium on the wall. Then looked again. It had changed. Five little figures were waving from the doorway. The three small ones were holding a home-made welcome home banner.

Elsie smiled, closed the bedroom door and skipped downstairs.

'All done,' she said, coming into the kitchen. 'I'm going home now.'

'Right,' said Magenta. 'You're taking the dog with you?'

'Yes,' said Elsie. 'Where's Corbett? I want to say goodbye.'

'Here,' said Corbett, poking his head through the window. 'I'm not speaking to *her*, though.' He nodded his beak towards Magenta. 'She brought me a *donkey*. What kind of rubbishy gift is that? It's not even bird related.'

'I know. But don't be cross. I'm going home now. High claw?'

Corbett held out his claw and Elsie smacked

it with her palm. Then she looked around the kitchen.

'Goodbye, Tower,' said Elsie. 'Thanks for all the cake.'

The tower gave a little shiver.

'Almost forgot! Your wages,' said Magenta. 'Twenty-one pieces of gold, right?' She handed over a large red velvet purse. It bulged in the most satisfying way.

'Thank you,' said Elsie. She pushed it deep into her cloak pocket. 'Will you say goodbye to Joey and Sylphine? Tell them I'll miss them.'

'Well, yes,' said Magenta. 'But you'll be coming back. You've made a good start, but there's a lot more to learn.'

'Of course she'll be back,' said Corbett. 'You will, won't you, Elsie?'

'Yes,' said Elsie. 'I rather think I will.'

'Until the next time, then,' said Magenta. 'I'll be in touch. Oh, there's a box over there for you. By the door. Open it when you get home.'

Much, much later, back in the attic above Pickles' Emporium, when all the hugging and kissing and talking and celebration and cries of delight over the purse of gold was over and everyone was asleep, Elsie did.

Inside was a pair of beautiful new blue shoes.

Acknowledgements

The terrific team at Simon and Schuster, especially my lovely editor, Jane. Ashley, my talented illustrator, who has brought Elsie's world to life. My good friend and fantastic literary agent, Caroline Sheldon. My always supportive husband Mo and daughter Ella. All my loyal readers, young and not so young. All the bookshops and libraries who buy this book. The cats who let me cuddle them whenever I get stuck.

Elsie and Magenta will be back!

Look out for Book Two
coming May 2018